LEMON RHYME READERS

Andy McLark
••• the Aardvark •••

By Kitty Higgins Illustrated by Robin James

Copyright © 1989 by Kitty Higgins and Robin James
Published by Price Stern Sloan, Inc.
360 North La Cienega Boulevard, Los Angeles, California 90048

ISBN: 0-8431-2742-2

Library of Congress Catalog Card Number—89-063488

Andy McLark had the chore
Of giving his brother a bath by four.
"Don't make a mess," his mother said,
"Just give him a bath and put him to bed."

So, Andy ran water into the tub,
Then added a sailboat and small pink sub.
Mike was next. He put up a fight,
Kicking and splashing with all his might.

Water went flying all over the place.
Andy got soap suds right in his face.
Mike whirled around, pushing the sub,
The water sloshed over the edge of the tub.

On hands and knees, Andy cleaned up the floor.
Mike threw a sponge. It went "splish" on the door.
He grabbed bubble bath from the edge of the tub
And sprinkled it over his little pink sub.

Mike said, "I'm tired of sailing this boat,
I wish I had something else that would float."
Without any sound, quietly as you please,
Mike slipped by Andy, who was still on his knees.

He ran down the hall—he didn't linger,
Straight to the fish bowl and stuck in his finger.
Then back to the tub, Mike plopped them in,
He couldn't wait to watch the goldfish swim.

Mike plugged his nose and ducked way down.
Andy pulled him up saying, "Be careful, you'll drown!"
He couldn't believe the sight in the tub,
Three fish blowing bubbles, BLUB, BLUB, BLUB.

Bubbles, blue bubbles, everywhere.
Little Mike popped them as they rose in the air.
Andy reached for a towel to dry his face,
There was a tube on the shelf in the towel's place.

Squiggly lines of toothpaste spread
All over the top of poor Andy's head.
There was toothpaste, bubbles and water galore.
Andy slipped in a puddle and fell on the floor.

By now little Mike had crawled out of the tub
To powder his sailboat and small pink sub.
Andy shook his head as he untied his shoe.
He had an idea, he knew just what to do.

It didn't take long to clean up the mess,
Then he took off his socks and began to undress.
Andy would have rather been riding his bike,
But instead took a bath with three goldfish and Mike.